THE ILLUSTRATED
FATHER GOOSE

First published in Canada by
Little, Brown and Company (Canada) Limited
148 Yorkville Avenue,
Toronto, Ontario
Canada M5R 1C2

Canadian Cataloguing in Publication Data

Tanaka, Shelley
The Illustrated Father Goose
ISBN 0-316-52709-2

1. Lishman, Bill – Juvenile fiction.
2. Geese – Ontario – Nestleton – Juvenile fiction.
3. Geese – Migration – Juvenile fiction.
I. McGaw, Laurie. II. Title

PS8573.I85F3 1995   jC813' .54   C95–931440–7
PZ7.L57Fa 1995

Design and Art Direction: Gordon Sibley Design Inc.
Project Editor: Mary Adachi
Color Separations: Batten/Cyber
Printing and Bindery: Friesen Printers

All photographs are © Lishman Duff, except photograph of
Bill and Carmen on page 47, which was photographed by Murray Skuce.

Printed in Canada

THE ILLUSTRATED
FATHER GOOSE

BY SHELLEY TANAKA
ILLUSTRATIONS BY LAURIE McGAW

LITTLE, BROWN AND COMPANY (CANADA) LIMITED

Boston • New York • Toronto • London

Prologue

"Is this a good one, Dad?" Carmen held up the pointy black mushroom she had picked. They were collecting morels in the old apple orchard near their home on Purple Hill.

"The light-coloured ones are better for eating. Try looking under the trees," her father said.

It was early May, a beautiful time of year in eastern Ontario. The spring frogs had already started to cheep. By bedtime they would sound like a chorus of sleigh-bells. The red-winged blackbirds were busy, too, screeching and flitting over the cattails.

Pepper the dog pounced in and out of the marsh, snuffled under bushes and poked her wet nose everywhere.

"There sure is a lot going on in the spring, isn't there, Dad?" Carmen said, swatting at an early mosquito.

"You bet. Our Canadian summers are short. Creatures don't have much time to build homes, look for food, and raise their families." Her father shaded his eyes and pointed at the sky. "Look!"

Carmen looked up. She couldn't see anything. But she could hear a noise. It sounded like a hundred yapping hounds.

The racket grew louder, until it was all around them. Then a flock of Canada geese burst out of the sky. As the birds flew overhead, the air was filled

with their wingbeats and honking cries. Carmen turned to her father. "How come they always try to make a V shape?"

"It's a very efficient pattern for flying. The lead goose breaks through the air, then the others ride on the wave behind it. The goose at the end of the line almost gets a free ride."

"That's not fair," Carmen protested.

"But they take turns. When the head goose gets tired, another bird takes its place. Everybody shares the work."

The V shape collapsed into a ragged W as birds fell out of formation and tried to catch up.

"Come on, geese, get back in line," Carmen called. "Where are they going, Dad?"

"North," her father answered. "They've spent the winter down south where it's warm and there's lots to eat. Now they're going north to raise their families. In the fall they'll fly south again."

"But how do they know where to go?"

"That's one of nature's mysteries. Perhaps they follow the position of the sun or the stars. Maybe they remember the patterns of the fields and rivers that they fly over. But part of it is tradition. The parent birds teach the young ones, and the information gets passed down from generation to generation. The same way Mum will one day show you how to make her famous rhubarb crisp, and you will pass that information down to your children."

"Don't you wish we could fly with the birds, Dad?"

Her father smiled. "You know something? That's always been my dream, ever since I was your age."

Carmen squinted up at her father. She could see flecks of grey in his bushy beard.

"Too bad you're a grown-up now," she said. "Did you know you're getting white hair already?"

Her father laughed. He shaded his eyes once more to look at the sky. The geese were already out of sight.

"I may be a grown-up, Carmen, but it's never too late. In fact, maybe it's time I started making that dream come true."

Learning to Fly

Carmen was waiting patiently with her mother and two older brothers, Aaron and Geordie. They were all staring at the strange creature standing at the top of the hill.

Pepper growled softly. Carmen scratched the dog's ears.

"It's okay, Pep," she said. "It's just Dad."

Bill Lishman was strapped into a hang-glider, his armpits held in a sling below the glider's flimsy wings.

Carmen shook her head and sighed. Her father was an inventor and metal sculptor who had once constructed a full-scale model of a lunar module. He'd even built a replica of England's giant stone circle, Stonehenge, using crushed automobiles. The Lishmans had a life-sized blue camel made of welded steel sitting at the entrance to their driveway, and Carmen was the only kid she knew whose refrigerator — one of her father's many inventions — magically rose out of the

counter at the push of a button.

She was used to her dad's crazy projects. Still, he had never tried to fly like a bird before.

Her father gave his family the thumbs-up sign and gripped the crossbar tightly with both hands. He screwed up his face and narrowed his eyes. Then he began to run downhill.

Carmen held her breath as he swept past. He ran faster and faster. He slowly lifted off the ground. The wings of the glider wobbled, but he hung on and then ...

CRASH! Down he came. The glider cartwheeled twice and landed in a clump of cedar.

Pepper was the first to reach the crash site. She rooted through the tangle of branches, metal and fabric until she reached the man beneath.

"Get your big nose out of my ear, you goofy dog!"

"Did you feel like a bird, Dad?" Carmen called out to the two long legs that poked out of the bushes.

"Not yet, Carmen," her father muttered as his head emerged through a tear in the wing. "Not quite yet."

Over the following summer Bill Lishman launched himself off that hill so many times that Carmen stopped counting. It was true that he was getting better — he had managed to stay in the air for several minutes — but he was still a long way from being able to fly.

Then he heard about a new kind of glider. It was called an ultralight, and it had a small engine with a propeller. It was noisy, but once you got off the ground, you could stay in the air for hours, gently soaring over the countryside.

For months after that, Carmen's father was in his workshop, welding and hammering together his own ultralight. He built a hangar nearby, and every morning he headed out for another practice session. Sometimes he dropped small presents for Carmen as he flew over the house. Once she'd got a new pair of sunglasses.

But there was always something to fix, some new improvement to make. Her father rebuilt the little plane so often that half the time Carmen didn't understand which version he was talking about, whether it now had two engines or one, pointy wings or square ones, three cylinders or four.

And he made crash landing after crash landing. On one test flight the engine quit right after take-off. The plane plopped down onto the end of the runway and caught her father's left foot under the wheel.

That was the worst time of all. Her father's plane was totally smashed, his broken foot was sore and swollen, and his mood was as cranky as a hornet's. Even Pepper stayed away.

"Aaron and I are taking the new plane out, Carm. Want to come? We've got an hour or so of daylight left."

Carmen was only too happy to take a break from her homework. She was trying to design a can crusher for a school science project, but every time she fixed one part, something else broke.

Down on the

airstrip sat the latest version of the ultralight. It looked like a wheelchair with a double set of wings.

Her father buckled himself into the pilot's chair. Aaron wound the propeller, and the noise of the engine shattered the twilight. The ultralight bumped down the runway. Then it lifted her father into the air.

Carmen watched him turn lazy circles over the fields. With his shiny helmet and goggles, he looked like a cruising dragonfly.

She wondered how the world looked from way up there. Did she look like a bug, too?

Then something else caught her eye. To the northwest she spotted the familiar formation of a flock of about thirty geese. They seemed to be flying towards her father.

Carmen and Aaron watched. Neither of them spoke.

Would this be the day that their father's dream came true? Could he fly with the birds?

The geese and the ultralight were alongside each other now, dark shapes against the sunset. Slowly the birds drew closer. Then, when they seemed to be just inches away from the plane's wing-tip, the V shape crumbled, and the honking geese scattered.

The ultralight circled again. This time it came in to land.

Carmen's father peeled off his goggles and rubbed his eyes.

"In this plane I can cruise at exactly the same speed as the birds," he said. "I can go wherever they go. But they're frightened by the noise of the engine. They won't fly with me."

"They just need to get used to you," Carmen said, patting her father on the arm. "Once they get to know you, they'll realize you're really a nice guy."

Her father looked at her closely.

"You're absolutely right. Why on earth would wild birds want to fly with this noisy contraption? I can't make them fly with me. They have to allow me to fly with them. To do that, I have to get them to accept me first. As one of the family."

Sister Goose

Carmen tried not to make a sound as she crept along the edge of the marsh. She and her dad had driven to a wildlife sanctuary north of Purple Hill. The sanctuary was located in an area where packs of coyotes preyed on the nests of Canada geese. The Lishmans had been given special permission to collect some eggs before the coyotes got them. Carmen hoped the geese would understand.

She hurried past a floating log. Finding the eggs was hard. The nests were well hidden, tucked into the reeds and bushes.

"Darn it!" Carmen stumbled to one knee as the mud sucked her rubber boot right off her foot.

She reached behind her to drag her boot out of the muck. As she did, she saw a sudden movement, low down, past the rushes.

She blinked. Had that log moved? She leaned closer into the long grass and stayed perfectly still.

There! The log slowly unfolded into a sleek, black neck. The goose had been lying low, hoping not to be noticed.

Carmen gently parted the reeds. The bird was sitting on a nest made of dead leaves, twigs and moss.

"Dad!" she called. "I've found one!"

A sudden thrashing erupted beside her. A huge gander reared up and spread its wings noisily, until it looked as big as she was.

Carmen's father was at her side in an instant.

"Get in the car," he said quietly.

Carmen slowly backed off. She climbed into the car and closed the door. Then she watched her father step away from the nest, his eyes never leaving the angry bird. When he was several steps away, he turned towards the car.

"Look out, Dad!" she screamed.

Her father crouched down just as the gander stretched its neck forward and attacked. Hissing in fury, it swept over him, its powerful wing barely missing his head.

Carmen's father scrambled into the driver's seat.

"That was scary," she said. "Did you get any eggs?"

He shook his head. "A rap from a gander's wing can cause broken bones. It's best to let those two keep their eggs."

"Will the coyotes get them?"

"Probably, but at least we're saving the ones we can." Her dad patted the picnic cooler in the back seat where thirteen eggs were snugly packed in foam. "If everything goes according to plan, that is."

Carmen and her father stood by the incubator in the workshop. Inside lay the mouse-sized eggs.

She picked one up and held it to her cheek. It was smooth and warm. She heard a chirping sound.

"I can hear them trying to come out!" She was bursting with excitement. For almost four weeks now she had been checking the temperature and humidity of the incubator every day. Away from their cosy nest and the warm protection of their mother, the eggs needed special care.

Now they were nearly ready to hatch. When they did, the baby geese would think the first creature they saw was their mother. Bill Lishman wanted that creature to be him.

Like magic, a tiny star shape appeared on one of the eggs. The star slowly blossomed, and the chirping sound became louder. Finally a pointy beak appeared.

It took ages for the goslings to hatch, and when they came out, they looked

more like baby dinosaurs than geese. They were bug-eyed and slimy, barely able to move.

"They don't look too healthy," Carmen said.

"Hatching out is hard work," said her father. "They're exhausted. But don't worry. A few hours from now they'll be downy little balls with big appetites and lots of energy."

"What's the matter with that one?" By the side of the incubator, one little hatchling was flopping around blindly. It couldn't seem to get the shell off its head.

"He looks as though he's wearing a helmet," Carmen laughed. "Can't we take it off?"

"We have to be careful. This one's taken so long to hatch that the yolk has dried. Now it's holding the shell on like glue." Her father gently tapped the shell to make little cracks. "We'll just give Egghead here some help so he can peck it off on his own."

Carmen looked at her father. He was having one of his Alfalfa Head days. With his rumpled hair, glasses, blue jeans and wool sweater, he made a pretty strange goose parent.

"I wonder if they think you're funny-looking?" she asked.

"I don't think children really notice whether or not their parents are funny-looking." He looked at Carmen sternly over the top of his glasses. "Or at least if they do, they are too polite to mention it."

"Come on, geese. It's time for a swim." With the goslings trailing behind them, Carmen and her father led the way to the pond.

Within days the birds had turned into bright-eyed fluffy bundles. They were still soft and small enough for Carmen to hold in her two hands, but each one already had its own personality.

Some were quite vain and preened themselves constantly. Some didn't seem to be very clever. Crash, for instance, had a habit of bumping into things. A few, like Igor, were always picking fights or getting lost. One of the troublemakers was named Christmas Goose. Carmen's father insisted that C.G. would become Christmas dinner if he got into any more trouble.

"Hey, guys. Wait for Egghead."

Carmen went back to rescue the smallest, who was being left behind again.

She picked him up and moved him to the front of the line. She tried to look annoyed as the other goslings quickly trampled their way over him.

"Heads up, everyone. Hole alert." She stepped over a pothole and stood to one side.

One after another the goslings flopped into the hole and then struggled to climb out, pumping their tiny wings and chirping furiously. When it was Egghead's turn, he stopped at the edge and poked at the gravel. Then, after several seconds, he walked around the hole. He might be small, but Carmen was sure that he was the smartest bird of all.

Down at the pond, they all threw themselves into the water. It was still very cold, but Carmen didn't mind. The goslings nibbled at her hair and scooted after waterbugs. Farther out, a few of them seemed to be trying to catch up with Pepper. The dog licked and nudged them as if she was their real mother.

Carmen took a deep breath and dove down to the bottom. She looked up at the rippled, sparkling surface. The goslings bobbed like plump little boats. Then they would suddenly turn upside down as they somersaulted into the water.

She popped to the surface, tickling their leathery black feet. The birds scattered, warbling excitedly.

Her father was standing on the bank. Some of the goslings were pecking at his toes. Except at night, when they were put into their pen, the birds followed him everywhere. If he stood up, they fell all over each other rushing to keep up with him.

"I guess they really think you're Father Goose now, don't they, Dad?" Carmen said, watching the goslings cluster around him.

"I think so."

"What does that make me, then?"

"Sister Goose?"

Carmen nodded. Then she held her nose and did a giant goose dive into the water.

Goose School

It was the middle of June, and the fields on Purple Hill smelled like wild strawberries. Carmen sat cross-legged outside her fort, a tiny cabin in the woods below the house.

Aaron and Geordie called the fort her outhouse, but Carmen loved it. She had a pot and a frying pan, a table, a candle, some incense and a sleeping bag. Her parents had said she could camp out here all night when school was over.

Carmen had just made lunch — bacon sandwiches and tea from the peppermint leaves that grew near the cabin. Pepper sat beside her. The bacon smell was driving the dog crazy.

Carmen tore off a small piece of sandwich for her. All around them the goslings began to bustle around and tug at her shoelaces.

"No people food for you," she said sternly. She held out a bunch of fresh dandelion leaves. Igor grabbed the whole handful.

Carmen let Pepper lick the bacon grease off her hands. She stood up.

"Come on, geese. Time for school. Father Goose is waiting."

"Are we going to teach them how to fly today, Dad?"

"We're not really going to teach them anything," her father answered. "They're born with the instinct to fly, although they won't actually be able to do so until they develop their adult wing feathers. But we do want them to learn to follow my lead and get used to the sound of an engine."

Carmen remembered the first time she had heard an ultralight engine up close. It had sounded like a dozen chainsaws all going at once.

"I don't think they'll like it," she said.

"That's why we're starting them with this." Her father turned and pointed to an odd-looking contraption parked beside the hangar. It looked like a miniature ultralight on a leash. Strapped to the frame was a portable tape recorder. Carmen's father turned it on, and the rumbling purr of a distant engine came from the black box.

The geese began to move around excitedly. Igor waddled up and pecked at one of the wheels.

"Hey, they like the sound," Carmen said.

"I call it the Goose Toddler. Come on, let's see if they'll follow."

From that afternoon on, Carmen helped her dad with the geese every day after school. First they let the birds out of their pen. Then they ran up and down the runway, pulling the Goose Toddler. The geese followed happily, pumping their stubby little wings as if they were already practising to fly. They didn't seem to want to stop.

A week later, Carmen arrived at the airstrip and found her dad sitting on a red motorcycle. The geese gathered around, eyeing it curiously. But as soon as he gunned the engine, they scattered as fast as their feet would carry them. Led by Igor, they scurried off the airstrip and headed for the pond.

"I think they'd rather be swimming, Dad," Carmen shouted as her father circled back. He climbed off the bike, and they both went down to the pond to round up the geese.

"Come on," Carmen begged. "Just drink a little more."

Egghead had a cold. The little gosling was in the kitchen, huddled in Pepper's old puppy cage.

Carmen held a spoonful of honey-water close to the gosling's beak. "Hey, hey, hey," she murmured, making the grumbly noise that the geese liked.

Egghead opened his beak and she slipped in the liquid. Then she rubbed his neck gently until he swallowed.

That night,

Carmen lay on her stomach, her chin leaning over the edge of the bed. From the cage on the floor beside her came a sad warble.

She got up and closed her door. The house was dark. The rest of the family was asleep.

She opened the cage and carried Egghead with her into bed. The little gosling pushed his head into the crook of her elbow, and they both fell asleep.

T he whole family worked hard to train the geese to follow the motorcycle. Usually Carmen ran behind them, calling "Come on, geese," and waving her arms to encourage them to chase the bike. But even with her, Aaron, Geordie, her mum and Pepper all running behind, the birds often headed down to the pond instead.

Still, after a while, they were finally getting the hang of it.

The geese had their adult wings now, and they no longer liked to be touched or patted. It was as if they knew that they had to keep each wing feather exactly in place if they were going to fly properly.

Sometimes Carmen sat on the bike behind her father. As the motorcycle increased its speed, the geese would actually take to the air. Carmen would lean her head against her dad's back and watch them flying beside her. They were so close, she could have reached out and touched their wing-tips. She could see

every feather in place, their strong necks pulsing, their beaks opening and closing as they breathed.

She wished then that they could all just take off together and soar into the sky, sailing over the fields and ponds, skimming the treetops, free to go wherever they wanted in that endless ocean of air.

The Big Day

Carmen stood beside the pen near the airstrip. Inside, the geese flapped and paced. They ignored their little wading pool that they normally loved, and instead hovered beside the gate.

For weeks now the geese had been practising. They'd flown perfectly beside the motorcycle, slowing down when it slowed, keeping pace with it as it turned. They'd even learned to follow the noisy ultralight while it taxied up and down the grassy runway. Now it was time for the real test.

The weather had finally cleared after several days of strong wind. The ultralight had been tuned up and checked over and over again. Everything was ready.

Strapped into the plane, Bill Lishman was nervous. He had already fumbled two take-offs.

For the third time he backed the plane up to the pen. He started the engine. Aaron and Carmen opened the gate, and the birds charged out in a flurry. The ultralight taxied to the runway.

"Come on, geese. Come on, geese," Carmen shouted as she ran behind them. Her arms were stretched out like an airplane, as she tried to herd them behind her father.

But it was no use. The birds, led by Igor, veered off and trotted straight to the pond.

The ultralight circled, landed and trundled back to the pen. Bill Lishman cut the engine.

"Guess where they went, Dad," Carmen said.

Her father sighed. "Okay, let's round them up."

It took forever to gather up the geese and walk them back to the pen. Christmas Goose was found a half-hour later, chasing ants outside Carmen's fort.

Then they went through the whole exercise once more. And again the geese headed straight for the pond.

By noon the wind was up, and it was too late to fly. Even the geese seemed subdued as they were put into their pen for the day.

"Carmelita." Her mother was shaking her gently. "Carmen, Dad's going to try to take the geese up again. Do you want to go down to the airstrip?"

Carmen opened one eye and looked at the clock. It was 6:00 in the morning.

"No, thanks," she muttered, turning her face to the wall.

"This could be the big day, you know."

"Who cares?"

Carmen rolled onto her back and stared at the ceiling. She was tired of the geese. She was tired of gas fumes blowing in her face as she ran behind the ultralight. Most of all, she was tired of getting her hopes up, only to have the silly birds run straight to the pond, or the wind to be wrong, or the dumb old plane to break.

Maybe she'd make some breakfast and watch cartoons. Looking after the geese had certainly been cutting into her TV time.

She got out of bed and wandered into the kitchen. Her mother and Geordie were out on the balcony. Carmen grabbed a bottle of juice and went out to join them.

The balcony was still damp with dew. Carmen shivered in her nightgown, even though it was July. Below them, at the bottom of the hill, her dad was backing the ultralight towards the pen, where Aaron waited by the gate. The sky was clear.

Bill Lishman looked up at the balcony and waved. He was ready to try again.

Carmen suddenly leaned over the railing.

"Wait! Wait for me!"

She ran into her room and pulled on a pair of jeans over her nightgown. She shoved her feet into sneakers on her way out the door and flew down the hill, flapping her arms.

"Here I come, guys!" she called. The geese flapped and cackled in greeting.

Her father revved the engine. He began to taxi down the runway. He was going faster than usual, as if he didn't want to give the birds time to think about heading anywhere else. Carmen and Aaron pulled open the gate, and the geese poured out.

The ultralight pulled into the air.

"Come on, geese!" yelled Carmen. "Fly!" And as she watched, the birds took off one by one. They were desperately trying to follow the plane, which was already far ahead of them.

"Wait for them!" she called to her father. He couldn't hear her, but he must have looked back, because the plane slowed down. He was flying very low.

As the geese struggled to catch up, the ultralight and the birds disappeared beyond the poplars to the south.

"Where are they? Can you see them?" she asked Aaron.

Her brother shook his head. "He's going pretty slow. Hope he doesn't stall."

Carmen strained her eyes. The sky was empty. Were the geese still with the plane? Had they doubled back and gone to the pond?

She waited. A million years passed. Then she heard it.

The nose of the ultralight appeared above the treetops. As the wing-tips came into view, they were followed by a broken string of honking, flapping geese.

Their geese. They were following her dad, their adopted parent. Father Goose was flying with the birds.

Carmen leapt up and down on the runway, waving her arms and screaming until she was hoarse.

As the plane came in, the geese flew lower and closer, their feet dangling from their broad, flat bellies. They came down like fluttering leaves, tumbling out of the sky. Then they glided in for a landing.

Everyone clustered around her father, taking pictures, shooting videos and cheering. The geese stretched their necks and bobbed. They waddled over to join in the celebration. They pecked at the ultralight with their glossy beaks, as if they were inspecting it. Igor found the flying licence and dropped it in her father's lap. They were all very pleased with themselves.

"Congratulations, Bill. You've done it!"

"Who's coming back to the house for breakfast?"

"Going to take a well-deserved break now?"

Carmen edged up to her father. She knew the question she wanted to ask.

"What happens now, Dad? What's next?"

Her father gave her a big hug.

"Next, Carmen, comes the hard part."

Operation Migration

"But *why* can't I go?" Carmen asked for the third time, as she and her parents walked to the airstrip. "Geordie could drive me to New York. I could meet the trailer there and drive to Virginia with the land crew while you and Joe fly with the geese. You know they won't settle down properly in their pen without me."

Her father sighed. It was six o'clock in the morning and the sky was still dark, but Carmen could see deep lines around his eyes. He had been up since two, getting ready for today's trip.

By now the geese flew beautifully with the ultralight. They formed a perfect V every time. The next plan was to lead them on a 400-mile journey across the Canada/United States border to a wildlife park in Virginia. The trip would take several days. A land crew had driven off in an old motor home the day before. They would meet the ultralight

at the end of each day to put the geese into their special pens for the night.

"You know why you can't go, Carm," her father said. "It's the middle of October. You have school. And I could be away for a long time."

"How come you have to take the geese on such a long trip? Why can't we just keep flying with them around here? This is their home. They're safe here."

"In the wild, Canada geese are migratory birds. They spend their winters in the south and summers in the north. But our geese, and many others that have been raised in captivity, don't know how to migrate.

If we can show them where to go, and if they can later follow the route on their own, maybe we can do the same thing for other birds, to help endangered species build up their populations."

"But they have to fly over a big lake. They've never done that before. What if they get tired? Where will they land? What if something goes wrong with the plane?"

Her father frowned. "We'll have rescue boats standing by below. But you're right. It is risky. We'll all just have to keep our fingers crossed."

The airstrip was very busy. Car headlights made odd shadows on the runway. Reporters were trying to take pictures. Neighbours had gathered on the hill to watch. Joe Duff, her father's flying buddy, was scraping frost from the ultralight. It was a new plane, a sleek model that looked like a prehistoric bird. Joe would be flying in a second plane behind the geese, ready to spot trouble or herd in any stragglers.

In their pen, the geese were bobbing and cackling noisily. Several of them preened their feathers. It was as if they were getting their wings ready to fly, too.

Bill Lishman was bundled up in big boots, silver mitts and a special black suit with a fur collar. He looked a bit like an astronaut.

Carmen handed him the rest of his gear. Smoke flares to signal for help. A radio transmitter. A bright orange life vest. It was all in case of an emergency, like a crash landing into icy Lake Ontario.

She sure hoped her dad wouldn't have to use any of this stuff.

The sky was brighter now, but cloudy. To the south lay a low line of dark-grey clouds. Was that a storm over the lake?

Her father wedged himself into the pilot's seat. Geordie opened the pen, and the geese came tumbling out. The ultralight taxied down the runway. It moved very slowly, heavy with a full tank of fuel and so much extra equipment.

Then they were off. The birds looked like shimmering kite tails strung from the plane's wingtips as they headed over the forest and out of sight.

Suddenly, Carmen's sharp ears heard a sound coming from the trees.

"What's that?" she asked Geordie.

"I don't hear anything," her brother said. "Come on. Let's get back to the house. We've got time for pancakes, with bacon."

But Carmen had definitely heard something.

"There. There it is again. You must have heard that one."

Geordie sighed and turned to his sister.

"It's gunshots, Carm. Hunting season has started."

All week Carmen worried. She worried about hunters. She worried about her father and the geese plunging into the lake. She worried about them getting caught in power lines. Even if they made it across to New York State, would they have enough strength to fly over the Appalachian Mountains?

She imagined Egghead being kidnapped by a flock of wild geese. She thought of Crash, who had a habit of flying into hydro poles. She even worried about Christmas Goose, who had dropped out of many practice flights and had to be fetched by truck and driven home.

But even as she worried, Carmen liked the idea that her geese were on such a momentous journey. They were flying from Canada into the United States, seeing mountains, forests, farms, lakes and rivers.

And everywhere the birds flew, people were pouring out of their houses to watch. Cars were stopping on the highway. Even the early pioneers had stopped their work when the geese flew overhead, filling the air with their heart-stopping cries.

At last came the call she was waiting for. Five days after setting off from Ontario, her father and the birds touched down at Airlie, Virginia, where they would all spend the winter. The geese would live in the park's three thousand acres of meadows, ponds and marshes. Her dad would stay in a poky little trailer so that he could take the geese on practice flights.

In the spring, maybe they would remember the route they had taken. Maybe they would be able to retrace their path and come home on their own.

Carmen leaned against the kitchen door and watched her mother plant tomato seeds. The damp, earthy smells of early April drifted in through the screen.

"Has Dad called yet?" she asked her mother. "Are they on their way home? If he doesn't come soon he'll miss mushroom season." She knew that if the geese didn't start for home on their own, her father and Joe Duff would lead them back with the ultralights.

Paula Lishman put down her trowel. She looked straight at Carmen. "When your dad went to round up the geese to lead them home, they had disappeared."

"Does that mean they're coming on their own? Can't he just find them and follow them back?"

Her mother frowned. "He's tried. He and Joe packed up the planes and retraced their flight south. They've checked every single spot they stopped at on their way down. No one has seen them."

"Maybe people just didn't recognize them. Lots of geese are flying north right now."

"Ours look different. They've all got big bands on their necks. They can't be mistaken for another flock."

Carmen didn't say anything. She whistled for Pepper and went outside. They wandered down to the airstrip.

The runway was covered in soggy puddles. The hangar was empty. Ice had made a big crack in the birds' wading pool.

Suddenly, Pepper became very still. The dog's ears pricked up.

They were coming from the southwest, over the poplars. It was geese, all right, but it couldn't be their birds. There were too many.

Carmen shaded her eyes. The huge flock came closer. They were flying very low. The air filled with the sound of cries and wing-beats. It was a wild flock.

Then she noticed that some of the geese looked odd. They had rings around their necks. The rings looked like grey soup cans.

Neckbands! Their geese had come home.

In a grand flurry the geese tumbled in for a landing. The tame ones came up to her, gabbling and yapping. Igor strutted and cackled proudly. Egghead pecked at her shoelaces and her jacket.

Carmen's eyes prickled. She was so happy she couldn't speak.
Then she found her voice. She turned and raced for the house,
the geese following in an excited babble.

"Mum, Mum!" she shouted. "Phone Dad, quick!
They're back!"

Epilogue

People have always wanted to be able to fly like the birds. In the Greek myth, Icarus tried to fly with wings made of wax. His experiment turned to disaster when he flew too close to the sun, and his wings melted. One hundred years ago, air pioneers first tried to fly by hanging from gliders, but many of their attempts ended in tragedy, too.

Then the Wright brothers made their first powered airplane flight in 1903. From then on, the aim was to fly faster, higher and farther. Few

people, it seemed, still longed for the quiet, soaring flight of the birds.

Bill Lishman's dream to fly with the birds turned into a mission to save them. When his geese returned to Ontario on their own, they proved that they could learn a migration route simply by being led over it once. If other species can do the same thing, we may be able to help two of the largest flying birds in the world — the whooping crane and the trumpeter swan.

In the 1800s, there were so many whooping cranes that huge flocks practically blocked out the

sun as they flew overhead. But overhunting nearly wiped them out, leaving only fifteen birds in North America by 1941. At present there is just a single wild population of about 150 birds. They spend the winter in Texas, and every year they journey to their summer home in the Northwest Territories, almost 2,500 miles away. Their trip is long and dangerous. Such a small group cannot afford to lose many individuals.

The trumpeter swan is in better shape than the whooping crane, but it is still rare. It, too, used to be plentiful, but it has almost disappeared from eastern Canada. Wildlife officials are trying to breed the birds in captivity and then release them into the wild. These released birds, however, do not know how to migrate south for the winter. So they stay in the cold north, where they struggle daily to find food and open water and escape capture by owls, coyotes, wolves and weasels.

Birds have been on this planet for millions of years. But in the past few hundred years, humans have interfered greatly with their traditional way of life. We've taken over their homes to make room for our cities, roads and farms. Pesticides and acid rain are destroying their habitat and food supply. We've hunted birds like the whooping crane and trumpeter swan for their quills, meat and down feathers, almost to extinction. And once a creature is extinct, there is absolutely nothing that can bring it back.

Now it is time to try to repair the damage. Perhaps species like the whooping crane and trumpeter swan can be reintroduced to their traditional breeding grounds. If they can then be shown how to migrate to a safe winter home, the birds can pass this knowledge on to future generations.

In time, the careful, persistent efforts of people like Bill Lishman may help us understand more about the mysteries of bird migration. They may help us give the birds back some of what we have taken away.